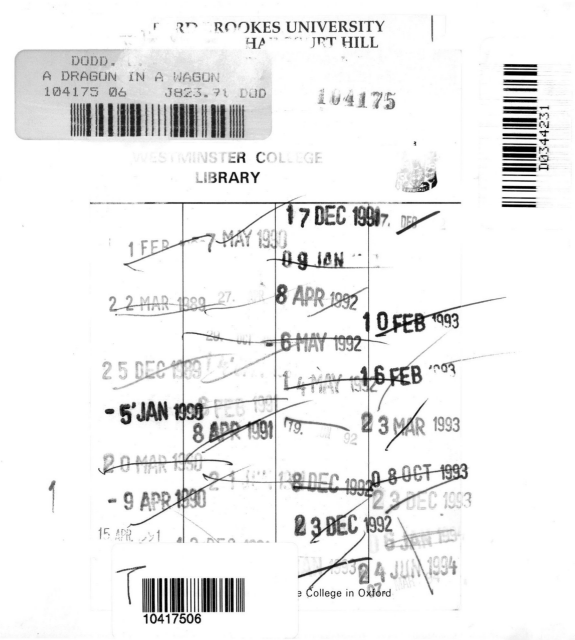

1

a·Dragon·in·a·Wagon

Lynley Dodd

Spindlewood

Susie Fogg
took Sam her dog
along by Jackson's Stream.
And as they walked
Susie talked,
and dreamed a wishful
dream.

'Sam,' she said,
'You're very good,
you never bark or bite.
The holes you dig
are not TOO big,
and you're always home
at night.
But just for once
it might be fun
if you changed from dog,' she said.
'To something HUGE
or something FIERCE
or something ODD
instead.

Let me see,
you could be...
a dragon
in a wagon,

a bat
with a hat,

a snake
eating cake,

a gnu
with the 'flu,

a whale
in a pail,

a giraffe
with a scarf,

a chimp
with a limp,

a yak
on his back,

a moose
on the loose,

a lizard
in a blizzard

or a shark
in the dark.'

A mossy log
tripped Susie Fogg,
she tumbled to the ground.
And as she wiped off
all the mud,
she looked behind
and found...

No sharks, no bats,
no hairy yaks,
no dragons in a jam.
Just the face,
the friendly face,
the DOGGY face
of Sam.